# TEENAGE MUTANT NINJA TURTLES
## BOOK III

**Kevin Eastman and Peter Laird**

and

**Dave Sim**

**Steve Lavigne**
LETTERS and COLORS

Teenage Mutant Ninja Turtles®: Book III

Teenage Mutant Ninja Turtles® TM and © 1987 Mirage Studios.
Cerebus TM and © 1987 Dave Sim.
Teenage Mutant Ninja Turtles®: Book III © 1987 First Publishing, Inc.
under exclusive license from Mirage Studios.

All rights reserved, including the right to reproduce this book or any portion thereof in any form whatsoever. The stories, incidents, and characters mentioned in this publication are entirely fictional. No actual persons, living or dead, without satiric content are intended or should be inferred. Cerebus is a trademark of Dave Sim. Teenage Mutant Ninja Turtles®, Raphael™, Leonardo™, Michaelangelo™, Donatello™ and all other prominent characters featured in this publication are trademarks of Mirage Studios.

Cover painting by Kevin Eastman.


Published by First Publishing, Inc.
435 N. LaSalle, Chicago IL 60610

ISBN: 0-915419-28-9

First Printing: December, 1987
Second Printing: June, 1988
Third Printing: March, 1989

6  7  8  9  0

Printed in the United States of America


Rick Obadiah, Publisher    Larry Doyle, Managing Editor
Kathy Kotsivas, Operations Director    Laurel Fitch, Editor
Ralph C. Musicant, Financial Director    Alex Wald, Art Director
Kurt Goldzung, Sales Director    Michael McCormick, Production Manager
Rich Markow, Editorial Coordinator

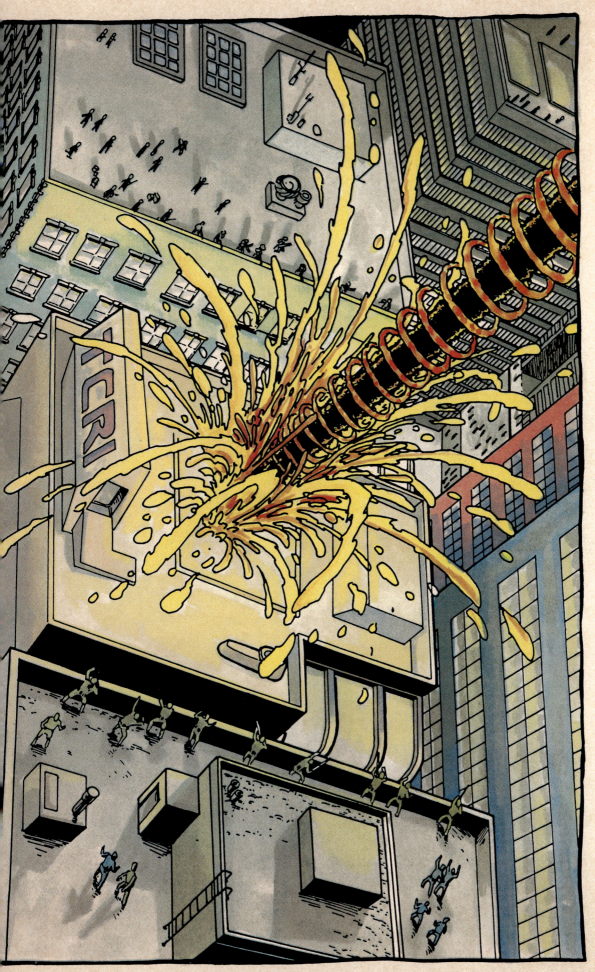

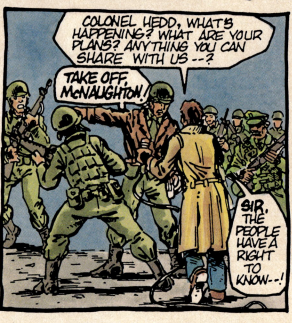

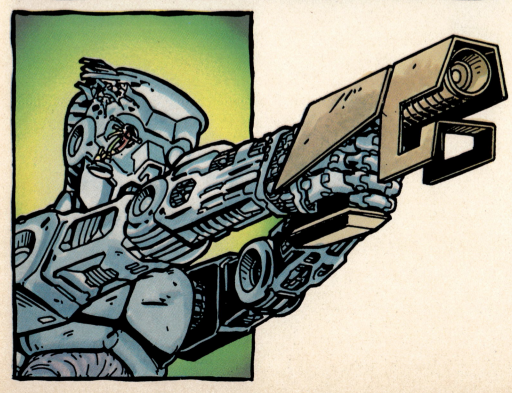

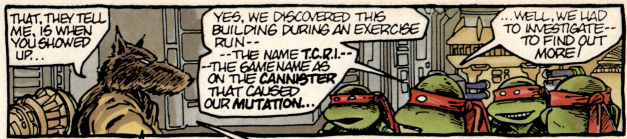

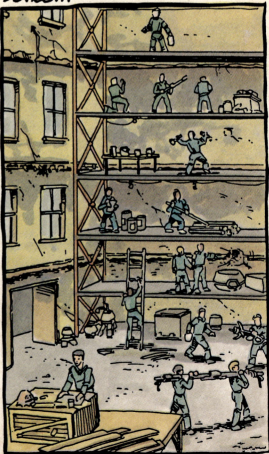

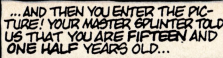

...MOMENTS LATER, SPLINTER FOLLOWED, AND FOUND YOU ALL ALIVE AND UNHURT, AND COVERED WITH THE GLOWING OOZE THAT HAD LEAKED FROM THE CANNISTER.
GATHERING YOU UP INTO A DISCARDED COFFEE CAN, SPLINTER WAS HIMSELF EXPOSED TO THE SAME SUBSTANCE--
A MUTAGENIC AGENT WHICH CAUSED YOU ALL TO CHANGE INTO WHAT YOU ARE TODAY!

MEANWHILE, WE HAD SUCCESSFULLY REESTABLISHED HYPER COMMUNICATION WITH OUR HOME PLANET. AS WE HAD SURVIVED AND ADAPTED SO WELL TO THIS WORLD'S WAYS, OUR LEADER ASKED US TO STAY ON AND CONTINUE OBSERVATION OF YOUR WORLD.

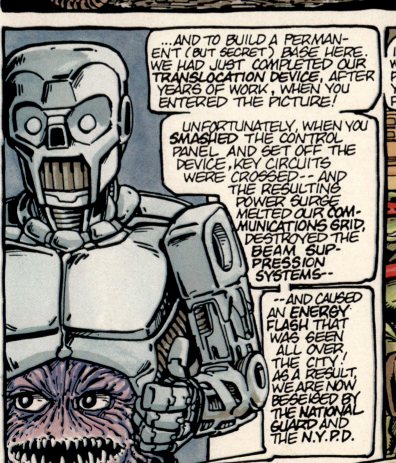

...AND TO BUILD A PERMANENT (BUT SECRET) BASE HERE. WE HAD JUST COMPLETED OUR TRANSLOCATION DEVICE, AFTER YEARS OF WORK, WHEN YOU ENTERED THE PICTURE!

UNFORTUNATELY, WHEN YOU SMASHED THE CONTROL PANEL AND SET OFF THE DEVICE, KEY CIRCUITS WERE CROSSED-- AND THE RESULTING POWER SURGE MELTED OUR COMMUNICATIONS GRID, DESTROYED THE BEAM SUPPRESSION SYSTEMS--

--AND CAUSED AN ENERGY FLASH THAT WAS SEEN ALL OVER THE CITY! AS A RESULT, WE ARE NOW BESIEGED BY THE NATIONAL GUARD AND THE N.Y.P.D.

WE'RE SORRY FOR OUR PART IN ALL THAT... BUT LISTEN-- WON'T THE FOLKS ON YOUR HOME PLANET DO SOMETHING TO HELP YOU? IF YOU'RE OUT OF CONTACT FOR A FEW DAYS, WON'T THEY GET WORRIED AND SEND HELP?

SADLY, NO... TO KEEP DISCOVERY RISKS TO A MINIMUM, WE ONLY COMMUNICATE WITH HOME ONCE EVERY THIRTY DAYS... AND, SINCE IT'S ONLY BEEN ELEVEN DAYS SINCE OUR LAST MESSAGE...

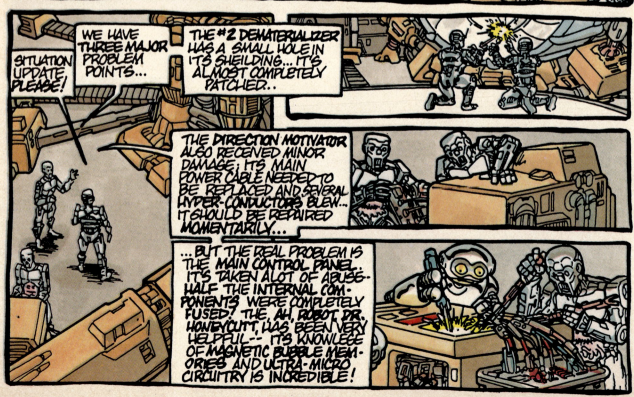

"ALMOST COMPLETE, LEONARDO-- JUST A FEW MORE MICRO-WELDS TO MAKE... A MINUTE OR TWO MORE..."

"MONITOR STATION TO COMMANDER-- FIRST FLOOR DEFENSE 'BOTS ALMOST OVERRUN... HUMAN TROOPS ARE ADVANCING TOWARD STAIRWAY TO UPPER LEVELS!"

"GO TO CRISIS CONDITION FIVE..."

"ALERT ALL STATIONS-- THE DEVICE IS ALMOST OPERATIONAL!"

"ALL PERSONNEL, REPORT TO TRANS-LOCATION AREA!"

"BEGIN WITHDRAWAL PROCEDURES-- ABANDON EXOSKELETONS!"

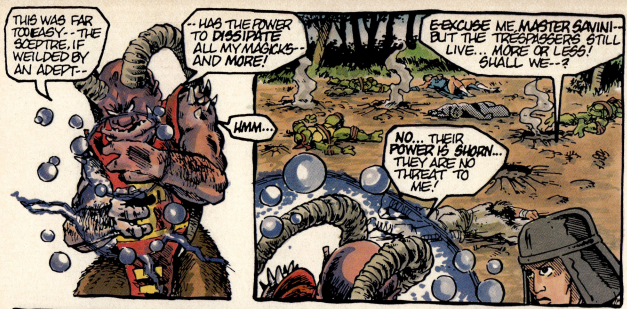

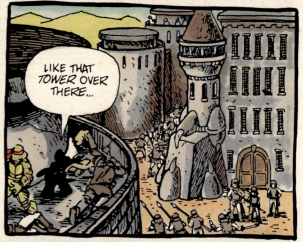

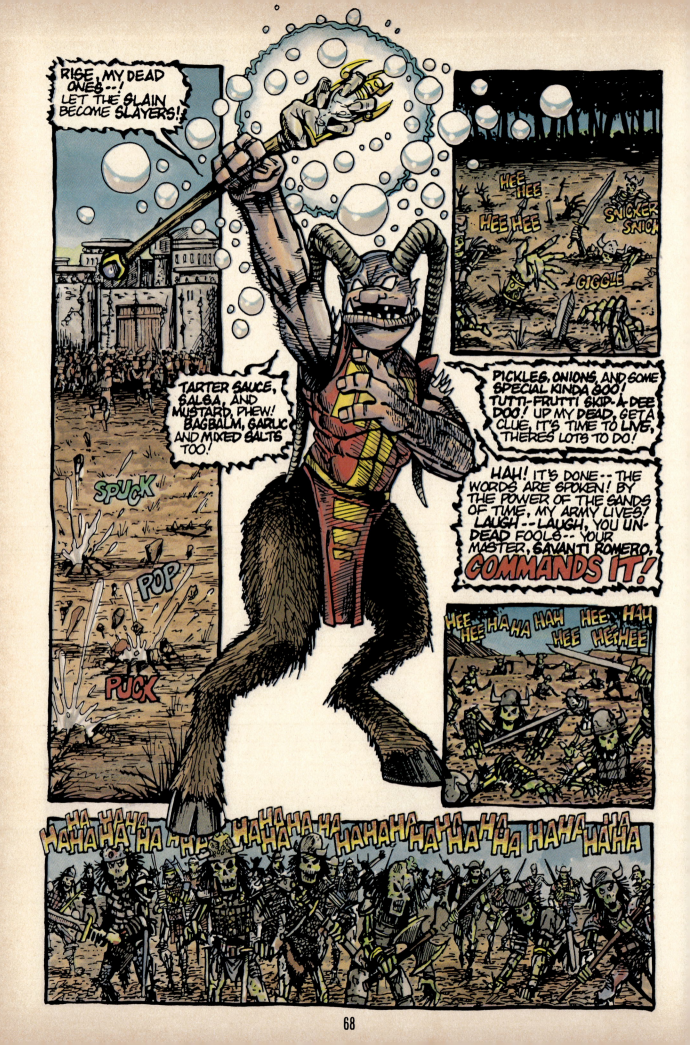

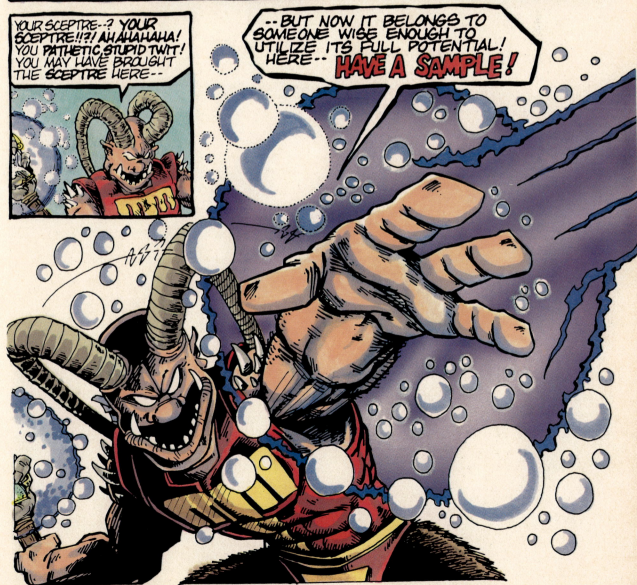

# EPILOGUE

# EASTMAN and LAIRD'S

## PRE-TEENAGE MUTANT NINJA

# TURTLES

## THE PASSING

STORY BY EASTMAN and LAIRD · PENCILS BY MICHAEL DOONEY
INKS 'N' TONES BY EASTMAN, LAIRD, DOONEY, RYAN BROWN and JIM LAWSON · LETTERS BY LAVIGNE

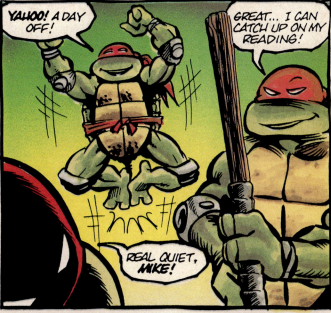

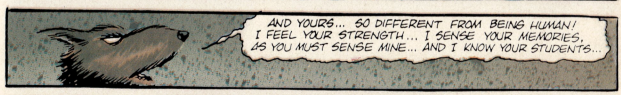

CHA-CHAK!

SPLOOSH!

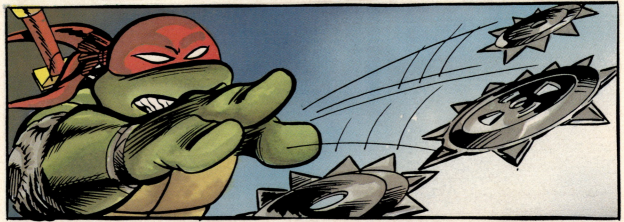

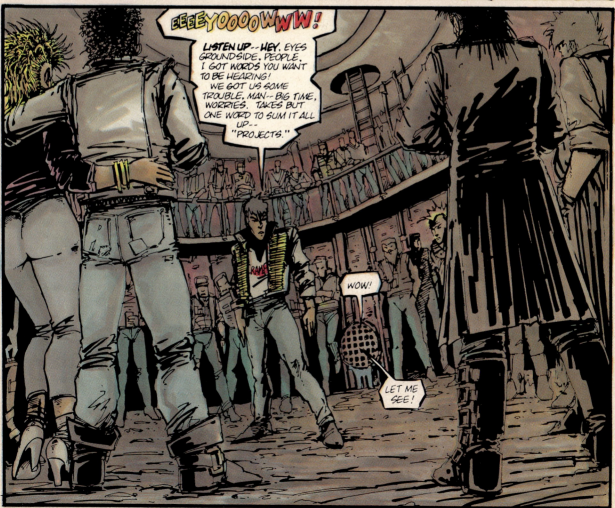

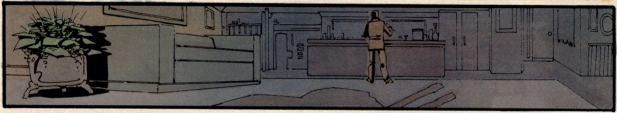

# PHANTOM FIGHTER

## GET BIGGER KICKS FIGHTING PHANTOMS!

Phantom Fighter is the martial arts game with a *big* difference. It's the new action game that lets you chop and kick against ghostly enemies with supernatural powers! These zombie phantoms get even bigger and stronger as your skill improves. (But don't worry—you've got some magic of your own.) You'll be challenged by some tricky questions. Ghosts, puzzles, and dialogue make this Kung Fu challenge more unpredictable. Get your kicks with Phantom Fighter!

- Over 100 Ghosts!
- Dialogue!
- Password Memory!

Licensed by Nintendo for play on the

Phantom Fighter™ is a trademark of Fujisankei Communications International, Inc., and is licensed by FCI for play on the Nintendo Entertainment System®. Nintendo and Nintendo Entertainment System® are registered trademarks of Nintendo of America Inc. FCI is a trademark of Fujisankei Communications International, Inc.

**Not Just Kid Stuff**

Fujisankei Communications International, Inc.
150 East 52 Street, New York, NY 10022
Tel. (800) 255-1431 In NY State (212) 753-8100
Phone Counseling Hotline (312) 968-0425